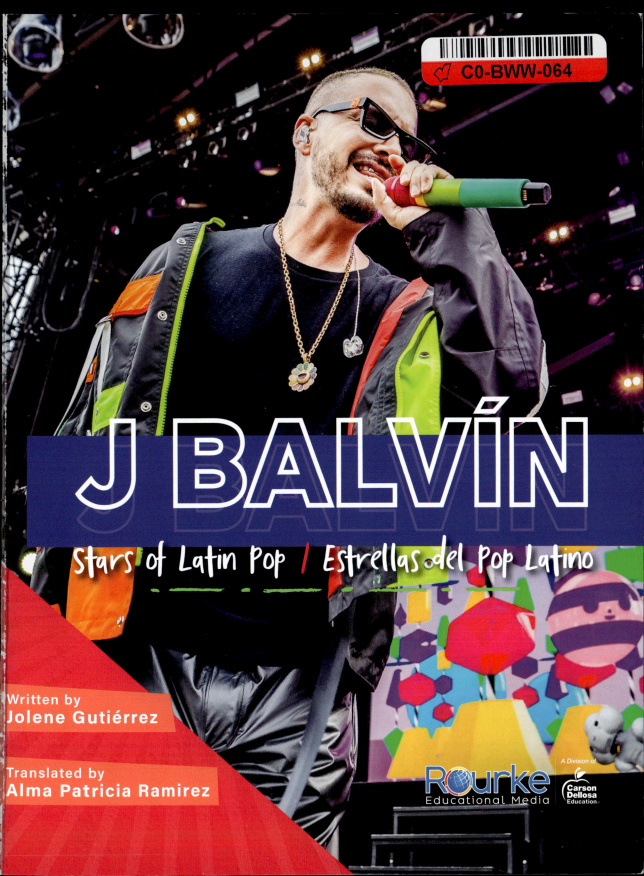

C0-BWW-064

J BALVÍN

Stars of Latin Pop / Estrellas del Pop Latino

Written by
Jolene Gutiérrez

Translated by
Alma Patricia Ramirez

Rourke
Educational Media

A Division of
Carson Dellosa
Education

ROURKE'S
SCHOOL to HOME
CONNECTIONS
BEFORE AND DURING READING ACTIVITIES

Before Reading: *Building Background Knowledge and Vocabulary*

Building background knowledge can help children process new information and build upon what they already know. Before reading a book, it is important to tap into what children already know about the topic. This will help them develop their vocabulary and increase their reading comprehension.

Questions and Activities to Build Background Knowledge:

1. Look at the front cover of the book and read the title. What do you think this book will be about?
2. What do you already know about this topic?
3. Take a book walk and skim the pages. Look at the table of contents, photographs, captions, and bold words. Did these text features give you any information or predictions about what you will read in this book?

Vocabulary: *Vocabulary Is Key to Reading Comprehension*

Use the following directions to prompt a conversation about each word.
- Read the vocabulary words.
- What comes to mind when you see each word?
- What do you think each word means?

Vocabulary Words:		Palabras del vocabulario	
• careers	• meditates	• carrera	• medita
• bankrupt	• networked	• bancarrota	• mercadotecnia
• marketing	• reggaetón	• hacer contactos	• reguetón

During Reading: *Reading for Meaning and Understanding*

To achieve deep comprehension of a book, children are encouraged to use close reading strategies. During reading, it is important to have children stop and make connections. These connections result in deeper analysis and understanding of a book.

Close Reading a Text

During reading, have children stop and talk about the following:
- Any confusing parts
- Any unknown words
- Text to text, text to self, text to world connections
- The main idea in each chapter or heading

Encourage children to use context clues to determine the meaning of any unknown words. These strategies will help children learn to analyze the text more thoroughly as they read.

When you are finished reading this book, turn to the next-to-last page for **After Reading Questions** and an **Activity**.

Table of Contents

Tabla de contenido

The Music Business
El negocio de la música

José Álvaro Osorio Balvín grew up near Medellín, Colombia. His parents didn't have **careers** in music, but singing and dancing were important to their family.

• • •

José Álvaro Osorio Balvín creció cerca de Medellín, Colombia. Sus padres no tenían **carrera** en la música, pero cantar y bailar era importante para su familia.

careers (ca-REERZ): people's jobs or work
carrera (car-rre-ra): empleo o trabajo de las personas

Venezuela

Medellín

COLOMBIA

Ecuador

Peru

When José was 12, his father gave him an electric guitar. José listened to bands like Nirvana and Metallica. José and two of his friends made a band. José said, "I always thought that I would have a future in music."

• • •

Cuando José tenía 12 años, su padre le regaló una guitarra eléctrica. José escuchó a las bandas de Estados Unidos como Nirvana y Metálica. José y dos de sus amigos formaron una banda. José dijo: "Siempre pensé que yo tendría futuro en la música".

The band Metallica inspired José to become a musician.

La banda llamada Metálica, inspiró a José a convertirse en músico.

Then José's life changed. His family went **bankrupt** when he was 14. José found jobs to try to help pay the family's bills. Around this time, he started calling himself "The Business." When José was 19 years old, he moved to New York City.

• • •

Luego, la vida de José cambió. Su familia se declaró en **bancarrota** cuando él tenía 14 años. José encontró trabajos para tratar de ayudar con las facturas que tenía que pagar la familia. Por ese tiempo, comenzó a llamarse a sí mismo "El negocio". José tenía 19 años cuando se mudó a Nueva York.

bankrupt (BANK-ruhpt): a legal process that can happen when a person or company owes more money than they have available

bancarrota (ban-ca-rro-ta): un proceso legal que puede suceder cuando una persona o compañía debe más dinero del que tiene disponible

Exchange of Ideas

José was an exchange student in the United States. He saw new ways to sell music. Hip-hop artists had clothing lines. Musicians were selling their CDs on the street.

● ● ●

Intercambio de ideas

José fue un estudiante de intercambio en Estados Unidos. Vio nuevas formas de vender música. Los artistas de hip-hop tenían líneas de ropa. Los músicos vendían sus CDs en la calle.

In New York City, José took jobs walking dogs and painting houses, but he still dreamed of being a musician. José says, "I followed that dream and after painting houses, I started painting my dreams."

• • •

En la ciudad de Nueva York, José tomó varios trabajos llevando a pasear perros y pintando casas, pero él todavía soñaba con ser músico. José dice: "Seguí ese sueño y después de pintar casas, comencé a pintar mis sueños".

New York City

The billboards he saw in New York City inspired José and provided him with ideas about how to sell and market his music in Colombia and around the world.

• • •

Ciudad de Nueva York

Las carteleras que él vio en la ciudad de Nueva York inspiraron a José y le proporcionaron ideas sobre cómo vender y comercializar su música en Colombia y en todo el mundo.

Coming Home

Regresando a casa

José liked the **marketing** ideas he saw in New York City. He realized that marketing would help his career. He brought those ideas home with him to Colombia. José began studying business in college.

• • •

A José le gustaron las ideas de **mercadotecnia** que vio en la ciudad de Nueva York. Él se dio cuenta que la mercadotecnia podría ayudarlo con su carera. Él se llevó esas ideas a su hogar en Colombia. José comenzó a estudiar negocios en la universidad.

marketing (MAR-ki-ting): trying to convince people to buy the product you're selling

mercadotecnia (mer-ca-do-tec-nia): tratar de convencer a las personas de que compren el producto que estás vendiendo

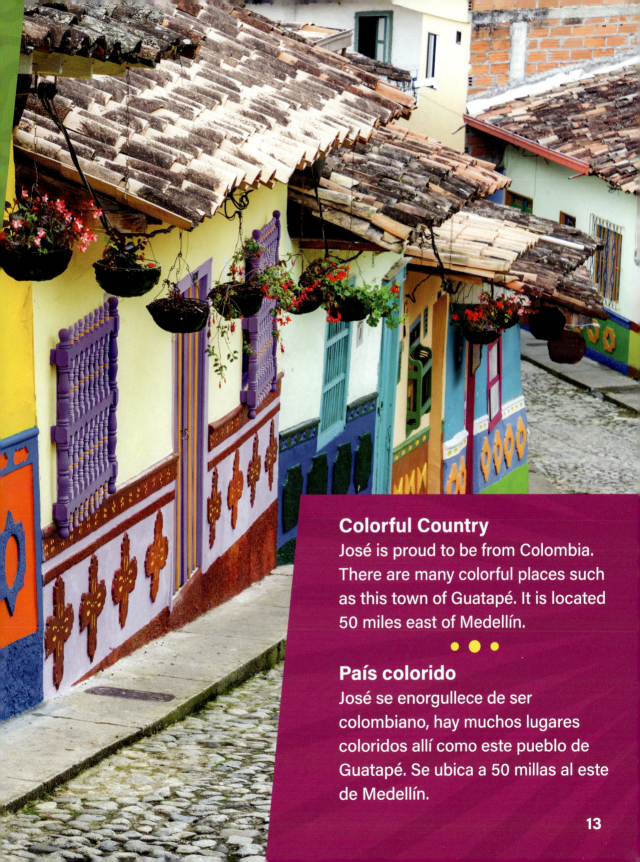

Colorful Country

José is proud to be from Colombia. There are many colorful places such as this town of Guatapé. It is located 50 miles east of Medellín.

● ● ●

País colorido

José se enorgullece de ser colombiano, hay muchos lugares coloridos allí como este pueblo de Guatapé. Se ubica a 50 millas al este de Medellín.

José also began performing **reggaetón** music. He called himself J Balvín. He made his own CDs to sell on the street. In 2004, he released his first single, *Panas*.

● ● ●

José también comenzó a cantar **reguetón**. Él se autonombró J Balvín. Él hizo sus propios CD para venderlos en la calle. En 2004, él lanzó su primer sencillo, *Panas*.

reggaetón (reg-ay-TONE): music influenced by Jamaican music, includes singing and rapping, usually in Spanish

reguetón (re-gue-tón): música influenciada por la música de Jamaica, incluye cantar y rapear, generalmente en español

J Balvín visited radio stations, performed at clubs, and shared his music on YouTube. He **networked** and got others excited about his music. His 2009 song *Ella me cautivó* won awards. He received his first recording contracts.

• • •

J Balvín visitó estaciones de radio, tocó en clubes y compartió su música en YouTube. Él se dedicó a **hacer contactos** e hizo que otras personas se emocionaran con su música. Su canción de 2009 *Ella me cautivó* ganó premios. Él recibió su primer contrato para grabar.

networked (NET-wurkd): contacted and shared information with other people

hacer contactos (con-tac-tos): ponerse en contacto y compartir información con otras personas

J Balvín speaks Spanish and English, but he routinely sings in Spanish. He says, "I want to be that guy to make Spanish music global." His goal is working! He's played at both Coachella and Lollapalooza Music Festivals. He was part of the 2020 Super Bowl halftime show.

• • •

J Balvín habla español e inglés, pero habitualmente canta en español. Él dice: "Yo quiero ser ese hombre que haga que la música en español sea mundial". ¡Su meta está funcionando! Él ha tocado en los festivales musicales Coachella y Lollapalooza. Él fue parte del espectáculo del medio tiempo del Supertazón 2020.

J Balvín performs with Jennifer Lopez at the Super Bowl.

J Balvín canta junto a Jennifer Lopez en el Super Tazón.

A Knack for Networking

J Balvín loves to network! He's worked with Beyoncé, Justin Bieber, Pitbull, Cardi B, and others.

● ● ●

El don de hacer contactos

¡A J Balvín le encanta tener una red de contactos! Él ha trabajado con Beyoncé, Justin Bieber, Pitbull, Cardi B y otros más.

J Balvín has received hundreds of award nominations. He's won awards at the Billboard Latin Music Awards, the Latin Grammy Awards, and the Latin American Music Awards. He received the Vision Award at the 2016 Hispanic Heritage Awards. At the 2020 Our Prize Awards, he won the Global Icon Award for spreading Latin music around the world.

• ● •

J Balvín ha recibido cientos de nominaciones para premios. Él ganó premios en los Premios Billboard de la Música Latina, los Premios Grammy Latinos y los Premios a la Música Latinoamericana. Él recibió el premio Visión en los Premios a la Herencia Hispana en 2016. En los Premios lo Nuestro de 2020, él ganó el Premio Ícono Mundial por difundir la música latina alrededor del mundo.

Global Grooves
J Balvín wants to share Latin music with the world. He says, "We want to elevate the culture and show that our sound is global."

● ● ●

Ritmo Global
J Balvín quiere compartir la música latina con el mundo. Él dice: "Queremos elevar la cultura y mostrar que nuestro sonido es mundial".

J Balvín poses at the 2019 MTV Video Music Awards.

J Balvín posa en los premios a los videos musicales de MTV de 2019.

Taking Care of "The Business"

Cuidando "El negocio"

The stressful life of a performer isn't always easy for J Balvín. He's dealt with panic attacks, anxiety, and depression. With the help of doctors, family, and friends, he has been able to improve his mental health.

• • •

La estresante vida de un cantante no siempre es fácil para J Balvín. Él tuvo que lidiar con ataques de pánico, ansiedad y depresión. Con la ayuda de los doctores, la familia y los amigos, él ha podido mejorar su salud mental.

J Balvín works to keep himself strong mentally and physically. He sees a therapist. He also **meditates**, exercises, and avoids alcohol and drugs. J Balvín also wants to help others with their self-care. That's why he helped create a free bilingual mediation program.

• • •

J Balvín trabaja para mantenerse fuerte física y mentalmente. Él ve a un terapeuta. También **medita**, hace ejercicio y evita el alcohol y las drogas. J Balvín también quiere ayudar a otras personas con su autocuidado. Es por eso que ayudó a crear un programa de meditación bilingüe gratuito.

meditates (MED-i-taytz): sits quietly and thoughtfully in order to be more mindful

medita (me-di-ta): se sienta en silencio y piensa profundamente para poder ser más consciente

A Colorful Calm

J Balvín calms himself with coloring books. "To me, colors are a universal language, like music." He shares coloring sheets with his fans through different organizations.

• • •

La calma de los colores

J Balvín se calma con libros para colorear. "Para mí, los colores son un lenguaje universal, como la música". Él comparte hojas para colorear con sus admiradores mediante diferentes organizaciones.

Another part of J Balvín's self-care includes fashion. He calls fashion his "life's passion, on the same level as music."

• • •

Otra parte del autocuidado de J Balvín incluye la moda. Él le llama a la moda la "pasión de su vida, al mismo nivel que la música".

Fashion Firsts

J Balvín thinks diversity should always be in fashion! He was the first Latino to make Nike Air Jordan 1 shoes. He was the first Latino to create fashion lines with GUESS. He was also the first Latin artist Fashion Week ambassador.

La moda primero

¡J Balvín piensa que la diversidad siempre debería estar a la moda! Él fue el primer latino que hizo los zapatos Nike Air Jordan 1. Él fue el primer latino que creó líneas de moda para GUESS. Él también fue el primer artista latino en ser embajador en la Semana de la moda.

27

By taking care of himself and doing what he loves, J Balvín is achieving his dreams. He says, "Dreams are the reason for everything I do. The reason why I get up. And the beauty of dreams is that they are infinite." What are your dreams? What are you doing to achieve them?

• • •

Al cuidarse a sí mismo y hacer lo que ama, J Balvín está logrando sus sueños. Él dice: "Los sueños son la razón para todo lo que hago. La razón por la que me levanto. Y la belleza de los sueños es que son infinitos". ¿Cuáles son tus sueños? ¿Qué estás haciendo para lograrlos?

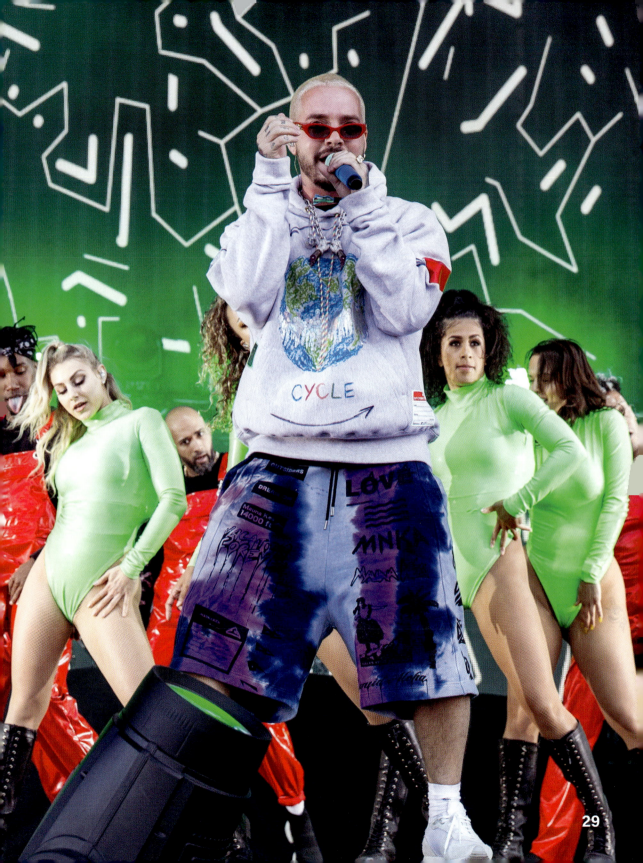

Index

After-Reading Questions

1. How has knowledge about business helped J Balvín?

2. What were some of the things J Balvín learned when he visited the United States?

3. How do you think J Balvín shows the world how important the Spanish language is to him?

4. How does J Balvín support his mental health?

5. What are some of the ways J Balvín has been involved in the fashion industry?

Activity

J Balvín takes care of himself by meditating, eating right, avoiding drugs and alcohol, and exercising. In addition to music, he finds joy through things like coloring books, helping others, and fashion. What are some of the ways you take care of your physical and mental health? What are some of your favorite hobbies? Create a weekly schedule and include times for things like exercise, meditation, work, study, and hobbies.

Índice

Preguntas para después de la lecturao

1. ¿Cómo ayudó a J Balvín el conocimiento acerca de negocios?

2. ¿Cuáles fueron algunas de las cosas que aprendió J Balvín cuando visitó Estados Unidos?

3. ¿Cómo crees que J Balvín le muestra al mundo lo importante que es el idioma español para él?

4. ¿Cómo mantiene J Balvín su salud mental?

5. ¿Cuáles son algunas de las maneras en que J Balvín ha estado involucrado en la industria de la moda?

Actividad

J Balvín se cuida meditando, comiendo bien, evitando drogas y alcohol y haciendo ejercicio. Además de la música, él se divierte con cosas como los libros de colorear, ayudar a otras personas y la moda. ¿Cuáles son algunas de las formas en que cuidas tu salud física y mental? ¿Cuáles son tus pasatiempos favoritos? Crea un horario semanal e incluye tiempo para actividades como ejercicio, meditación, trabajo, estudio y pasatiempos.

About the Author
Sobre la autora

Like J Balvín, Jolene Gutiérrez is following her dreams. She works as a teacher-librarian at a school in Denver, Colorado and connecting students with literature and sharing information are some of her favorite things. Learn more about Jolene, her writing, and her dreams at www.jolenegutierrez.com.

• • •

Como J Balvín, Jolene Gutiérrez está siguiendo sus sueños. Trabaja como maestra y bibliotecaria en una escuela en Denver, Colorado y conectar a los estudiantes con la literatura y compartir información son algunas de sus cosas favoritas. Obtén más información sobre Jolene, su escritura y sus sueños en www.jolenegutierrez.com.

Quote source: Borge, J., and S. Castillo. "Why You Should Add J Balvin to Your Playlist (Even Barack Obama Is a Fan!)." Oprah Magazine. March 20, 2020. www.oprahmag.com/entertainment/a28819811/who-is-j-balvin/; Burgos, J. "J Balvin Just Launched a Spotify Podcast Tackling Mental Health & His Path to Success." Remezcla. January 23, 2020. remezcla.com/music/j-balvin-podcast-spotify-made-in-medellin/; Cobo, L. "J Balvin Wants to Be Music's Next Billionaire." Billboard. February 27, 2020. www.billboard.com/articles/columns/latin/9323112/j-balvins-plan-to-become-musics-next-billionaire; Exposito, Suzy. "J Balvin's Latin Pop Crusade." Rolling Stone. Last modified May 7, 2018. www.rollingstone.com/music/music-latin/j-balvins-latin-pop-crusade-201922/; Morin, A. "J Balvin's Best Fashion Moments Prove He's Not Afraid to Be Bold." E! Online. Accessed May 31, 2020. www.eonline.com/news/1134495/j-balvin-s-best-fashion-moments-prove-he-s-not-afraid-to-be-bold.

PHOTO CREDITS: Cover: ©Ben Houdijk / Shutterstock; page 3: ©Daniel V. / Wikimedia; page 3: ©Jeff Pinilla / Wikimedia; page 5: ©Alejo Miranda / Shutterstock; page 7: ©4 PM production / Shutterstock; page 7: ©SMG/ZUMA Press / Newscom; page 9: ©Hayk Shalunts / Shutterstock; page 10: ©Branimir76 / Getty Images; page 11: ©Andrey Bayda / Shutterstock; page 9: ©Jess Kraft / Shutterstock; page 14: ©RM9/Rosie Mendoza/WENN / Newscom; page 15: ©SMG/ZUMA Press / Newscom; page 17: ©german eluniversal SUN / Newscom; page 19: ©Paul Kuroda/ZUMA Press / Newscom; page 21: ©Everett Collection / Newscom; page 23: ©J.M. HAEDRICH/SIPA / Newscom; page 25: ©Jerry Perez/PacificCoastNews/PacificCoastNews/Avalon.red / Newscom; page 26: ©Lev Radin/ZUMA Press / Newscom; page 27: ©LAURENT BENHAMOU/SIPA / Newscom; page 29: ©Daniel DeSlover/ZUMA Press / Newscom

Library of Congress PCN Data

J Balvín / Jolene Gutiérrez
(Stars of Latin Pop)
ISBN 978-1-73164-337-7 (hard cover)
ISBN 978-1-73164-301-8 (soft cover)
ISBN 978-1-73164-369-8 (e-Book)
ISBN 978-1-73164-401-5 (ePub)
Library of Congress Control Number: 2020945047

Edited by: Madison Capitano
Cover design by: Michelle Rutschilling
Interior design by: Book Buddy Media

Rourke Educational Media
Printed in the United States of America
01-3502011937